MY COLD KENTUCKY
HOME

MY COLD KENTUCKY
HOME

LORI A. MOORE

TATE PUBLISHING
AND ENTERPRISES, LLC

Published by Tate Publishing & Enterprises, LLC
127 E. Trade Center Terrace | Mustang, Oklahoma 73064 USA
1.888.361.9473 | www.tatepublishing.com

Tate Publishing is committed to excellence in the publishing industry. The company reflects the philosophy established by the founders, based on Psalm 68:11,

"The Lord gave the word and great was the company of those who published it."

Book design copyright © 2016 by Tate Publishing, LLC. All rights reserved.
Cover design by Norlan Balazo
Interior design by Manolito Bastasa

Published in the United States of America

ISBN: 978-1-68319-303-6
Fiction / Horror
16.02.24

This is the part where I'm supposed to say something sweet and dedicate the book to my husband and thank him for reading each piece of the book after I wrote it and for supplying me with adjectives when I couldn't think of them and stuff like that.

But I think I'm going to dedicate this book to Stephen King, best-selling horror and suspense author of about a million novels and short stories. Sure, he'll never read this book to know it's dedicated to him, and why should he? He's Stephen King, for pity's sake. He would read this book and shake his head in disgust wondering why I was killing trees to print this crap. Then I'd have to say, "But, Mr. King, this was my first time trying to write fiction, so cut me some freakin' slack, would ya?"

Acknowledgments

··················

Without family and friends who were interested in my writing, I would not have had the opportunity to write this first piece of fiction, this first novel where I could kill off characters named after the aforementioned family and friends, so I thank them profusely for the opportunity to make them literary victims. For any law enforcement officials reading this, please understand that if you find any of my family or friends deceased, I only killed them in words, not in deeds, so please don't come looking for me.

Contents

·················

Preface

....

I GREW UP in Jeffersontown, Kentucky, attended Jeffersontown High School, and have spent a great deal of time in and around that wonderful area. I have great memories of attending more than forty of the Gaslight Festivals, watching the Gaslight parades, walking through Skyview Park (before it became just a collection of baseball fields), and watching the gentle giant known as Big Lip Louie walk hundreds of miles up and down Taylorsville Road throughout the years.

This book has been an opportunity for me to highlight one of Kentucky's friendly towns, honor some of its history, and reference some things that the locals will remember. The characters and action in this story are purely fictitious. Any resemblance to actual events or real persons, living or dead, is purely intentional, err, I mean coincidental.

Prologue

NEWTON'S LAWS OF motion describe the relationship between a body and the forces acting upon it and its motion in response to those forces.

When Brunerstown was established in the late 1700s, it was a place where people came from miles around to purchase goods and use the services of the blacksmiths, potters, and other tradesmen.

Later renamed Jeffersontown, the city grew; and by the time the railroads were being developed throughout the south, Louisville, Kentucky, was a major hub, with tracks running through Jeffersontown and surrounding areas.

This is when Newton's laws of motion start to apply to what was going to happen in Jeffersontown for the next one hundred plus years as a result of the relationship of bodies, literally, and why one young girl would refer to her childhood house as "My Cold Kentucky Home."

1

THE LIAR'S BENCH

THE USUAL STORIES told on The Liar's Bench at Karem's Bait Shop are about the fish that got away, but today the story that Haskell is about to tell is one he has been wanting to get off his chest for many years.

Haskell is in his nineties and has lived in Jeffersontown all his life. Jeffersontown is a large "small town" of 26,000 plus residents in eastern Jefferson County, a suburb of Louisville, Kentucky.

Every Tuesday, for too many years to count, Haskell has been meeting his buddies Fred and Bud at Karem's to swap stories and reminisce about the past. They pine for the German chocolate Danish they used to get at Duke's Bakery and the home-cooked meals from Murphy's Restaurant. The three of them have spent way too many nights at The Maple Inn with enough hangovers and a few bar fights to make them worse for wear.

Haskell can remember when the building now housing the police department used to be the skating rink and when the lion got loose at Tucker Lake. Yes, Haskell has seen a lot happen in J'town throughout the years.

But what he's about to share now with his friends is something that's never been told.

2

THE HOUSE

The sun shines not on my cold Kentucky home,
'Tis dismal, and dreary, and gray,
Bad things happen here
And there is blood spilled on the floor,
Run now, while you can, and stay away!

ROBERT AND CONSTANCE Agee built the house in 1903 about four miles away from Henry and Rebecca Watterson, Jeffersontown's most famous residents. While it was nothing like the spectacular Mansfield Estate, the Agees jokingly named their property on Edington Avenue as well, calling it Hubertson, after Robert's grandfather. Nothing near the one hundred acres of Mansfield, Hubertson was comprised of a little under five acres on a dead-end street with plenty of privacy on all sides. On the dead end was the railway and to the rear an empty field.

The landscaping was the most impressive part of the Agee property. Sweet magnolia trees dotted the front lawn, lending a symbol of Southern charm to a state that was considered neither northern nor southern. Clusters of three-foot-tall peonies of all colors—red, white, and yellow—stretched across one side of the property. Beautiful cascades of brilliant yellow and white roses peeked out through a natural rock wall in front of the house. Along the side of the property adjacent to the railroad track were fruit trees: cherry, apple, and pear. Sometimes the occasional vagrant riding the rails would help himself to some of the fruit, perhaps his only meal for several days to come. At the rear of the property stood tall evergreens of spruce and pine, providing a natural fence and border to Hubertson.

The house itself was humble—a two-story frame house. Upstairs was three bedrooms, and downstairs was a parlor, a formal dining room, a kitchen, and a bathroom. The parlor and dining room shared a two-way fireplace. There was root cellar that could be accessed from inside the house in the entryway or service porch at the rear of the house.

Yes, from the outside, everything looked beautiful and normal.

But the house on Edington Avenue already had a history.

3

1912

AFTER LOSING THEIR first child to miscarriage, Constance and Robert Agee couldn't have been happier when little Emily was born. Emily was a smiling and happy child, though somewhat shy. With long brown hair, big brown eyes, slender, and with alabaster skin, Emily was very pretty and a girly girl who loved to wear dresses with lace and bows. She was the apple of her father's eye, and he was very proud of her, though he sometimes wished she would not be so awkward around adults because he wanted his family to make a good impression on the community.

Now eight years old, Constance and Robert were starting to worry because Emily was starting to wander around the five-acre property and be gone for hours before her parents could find her. They had told Emily over and over again to stay within their view from the house, but she was a curious child and liked walking through the trees and flowers on their land and often lost track of how long she'd been gone and far away she'd gotten from the house. She enjoyed the melodies of a multitude of singing birds she'd find in the expanse of her family's property and the wild flowers that were rampant along the fence line. She liked to head out before breakfast when there was still a light morning dew on the lawn burning off in the bright sunlight leaving little rainbow-speckled drops on the blades of grass. To Emily, it felt as though she was playing in a magical fantasia when she had this time alone in nature.

She seemed to be a gifted child intellectually, but she was easily overwhelmed or distracted by new situations, noises, smells, and situations going on around her. Her parents were trying to implement some structure and limits into her day as a way to help her manage her sensitivity.

Then the Agees really started to get concerned about Emily. Her bedroom was upstairs, the one nearest the stairs, and she would play in her closet for long periods of time. When they built that bedroom, there was an odd angle to the eaves in the front of the house, so there was a closet inside of the closet, so to speak, like a little cave, where Emily would crawl into from the main closet and play. When her mother asked Emily why she liked it in the little closet cave under the eaves, Emily said it was because she could hear singing there, and it was comforting. Thinking it was just the imagination of a little girl, Constance didn't think much more of it until Emily started to tell her parents that she could hear people talking in her bedroom.

Constance slept with Emily in her room that night to see if perhaps she was hearing something through the screened window and thinking it was someone in her bedroom, but neither she nor Emily heard any voices that night.

On many days after that, the Agees would find Emily on the back porch sitting in the rocking chair, smiling and telling her mom and dad and she was listening to the singing.

Robert knew that hearing voices could be associated with some medical or psychiatric conditions, but didn't think it applied in this instance and decided that they needed to nip this in the bud. He told his daughter that if she continued to make up stories about people talking and singing, they were going to have to punish her and she wouldn't be allowed to play outside the next day. After all, he felt that Emily was too old to be playing these pretend games and was worried what other people would think.

Robert knew he shouldn't be embarrassed by his daughter's behavior, but as a physician, he wanted to maintain a respectable reputation in the community. After all, he had big shoes to fill. Jeffersontown had always been fortunate to have great doctors in their community. Dr. William Bryan, who practiced medicine in J'town from 1819 until 1871, had been well respected, making rounds on horseback and even acting as a surgeon when needed.

Sometimes after church, Emily would run off to play in the German Reformed Presbyterian Cemetery down further on Watterson Trail, which was not dignified at all for the daughter of a doctor. His wife, Constance, was less worried about public appearances. While she knew it was a genuine concern for her husband, she felt it was the parents' job to help the kids explore their imaginations and creativity and allow them to be kids while they were young. She felt sorry that there were no young children nearby for Emily to play with and didn't mind her daughter inventing pretend people that she heard talking to her. Constance felt that Emily was a sensitive child, quick to show empathy for others but also quick to be hurt by another's unkind remarks.

Emily was devastated that her dad would think she was making up a story about hearing the music, the singing, and the people talking. It was real, and she didn't understand why her parents didn't hear it too. Why would they punish her for something she didn't do? How could she prove to her parents that she wasn't lying? Emily cried herself to sleep that night thinking that her parents didn't trust her and that she was a bad little girl.

The next day, Dr. Agee made good on his threat and didn't allow Emily to go outside. Emily was distraught and withdrawn and didn't utter but a few words during dinner with her parents. She had heard people talking outside but didn't say anything to anybody for fear of being further punished.

After dinner, Constance told Emily that she could sit on the back porch and read, but not to go outside. Emily took her favorite book, *Alice in Wonderland*, out to the back porch with her and plopped down in a chair, miserable. She couldn't read it all by herself, but there were bits and pieces that she could read on her own, and she liked the illustrations. Plus, she knew most of the story by heart anyway. It was her favorite book because her aunt Catherine from Cincinnati had given it to her and had written inside the front cover, "To my very pretty, dark haired, eight year old niece." Her mom and dad had gone into the parlor after dinner, leaving her alone on the porch.

Fifteen minutes later, Emily started to hear voices talking. Yes, it was definitely people having a conversation. It wasn't her mom and dad because they were in the parlor. She looked through the screened-in porch into the back lawn but didn't see anyone. She could still hear the voices. She walked over to the side of the house with the rows and rows of flowers. No one was there. Now the talking turned into singing.

It was a different kind of singing from what Emily was accustomed to hearing. This was a mournful, melodic style with which she was unfamiliar, but it resonated with her, and the rhythmic nature was somehow soothing. She remembered once going on a house call with her dad out to one of the farms to visit a sick patient and hearing a similar antiphonal song being sung by the workers in the fields. Her dad told her it was a type of song people sometimes sang when they worked to keep from being bored or to keep them in synch with each other as a team.

She looked out the other side of the porch, toward the fruit trees and the railroad track, still not seeing any people, but the singing was louder when she was on that side of the porch.

Figuring there must be people on the track that she couldn't see, Emily had an idea. She so wanted her dad to understand that she wasn't making up stories about hearing the singing, that if she could only find the people doing the singing and show them to her dad, he would believe her. She knew she needed to get down to the railroad tracks and find those singers.

Despite her mom telling her to not go outside, Emily was desperate to prove her innocence to her parents and eased the porch door open and slipped out back. As she walked down the hill from the side of the house to the railroad track, the singing grew louder and louder. Excited that she was finally going to be able to prove herself to her dad, Emily started to run toward the singing.

Mesmerized by the opportunity to find the source of the singing, Emily stepped onto the track just as the L&N

was making its way past the Agees' house. The conductor never saw Emily, and Emily never heard or saw the train as it plowed into the little eight-year-old's body, pitching her off to the right side of the track. She never even had a chance to scream.

Coming out to the back porch to check on Emily, Mrs. Agee was surprised to not find her there. She hadn't seen her pass the parlor to head upstairs to bed. She noticed that the porch door was slightly ajar. Frustrated that her daughter disobeyed her, she called to her husband to help her go outside and search for her.

Calling her name and walking the entire expanse of the property yielded no results, and it was past dusk, so the Agees were starting to worry about Emily. It was then that Robert noticed Emily's book, *Alice in Wonderland*, lying beneath the fruit trees. Surely she hadn't wandered down to the railroad tracks. Telling his wife to stay where she was, Dr. Agee walked down to the train tracks and looked left, then right. He saw something that caught his eye on the track up to the right, so he walked a few yards and found his daughter's shoe lying on the track. Panic setting in, he looked further and saw Emily's small body crumpled and lifeless on the side of the track ahead. Robert dropped to his knees and wailed.

The town was in shock when neighbors found Robert's and Constance's bodies hanging from the walnut tree in their backyard the next day.

Robert had carried Emily's lifeless body and placed it at the foot of the walnut tree before throwing two ropes up over a branch and tying nooses at the end of them. He then upended two oak buckets, helping his wife up on one and then stepping up on the other. As they took one last loving glance into each other's eyes, they heard singing coming from the railroad track. After Robert kicked out the buckets from beneath them, their bodies slid to the lengths of their ropes. Walnuts gently fell from the tree, landing as if making a blanket around Emily on the ground.

Dr. Agee had written a note and pinned it to his body before putting the noose first around his wife's neck and then around his own. The note simply read, "We couldn't live without our Emily."

The house had claimed three victims.

4
....

1978

Tommy rolled his '72 Ford Mustang quietly up the long driveway hoping no one would hear the after-market muffler. It was 2:00 a.m., and Tommy's dad had told him to be home by midnight. They had been arguing a lot lately, and Tommy just wanted to sneak in the house and go to bed without having to get into it with his dad.

After hanging out with his friends and performing with the audience alongside *The Rocky Horror Picture Show* at Vogue Theatre on Lexington Road, Tommy and his friends had decided to head out just past J'town to test their courage. Legend had it that beneath the Southern Railway Trestle dwelt the Pope Lick Monster, named after the creek and road running nearby, just off Taylorsville Road. Nearly all teenagers in the county had heard of the half-man, half-goat who allegedly lived beneath the trestle and would attack visitors who dared invade his space. Not stupid enough to actually attempt to climb the one-hundred-foot trestle and be stuck somewhere along the massive stretch of track with nowhere to go in the event a train came, the boys instead drove beneath the trestle, slowly hoping to catch an image of the goat man. The Pope Lick Monster was supposed to be some former circus freak who was the only survivor of his troupe's train derailment and had taken up residence beneath the trestle. But luck wasn't with them tonight, or perhaps it was, as they were unable to get any glimpses of this legendary menace. Still not ready to go home yet, the trio drove past the old Henry Watterson mansion that had burned down two years earlier to see if they could get any spooky vibes but, upon failing there as well, decided to give up and go home.

Like all dads, Karl Richter just wanted what was best for his son. He and his wife had divorced two years earlier, so it was still an adjustment to being a single parent. Now that Tommy was a senior in high school, Mr. Richter wanted to ensure that Tommy had a career to go into that would be secure and provide for him and hopefully a future family. Tommy had dropped the bomb a few months earlier that he wasn't going to consider college after graduation and intended to pursue a career as an actor.

Karl was just third-generation American. His grandfather had moved to the United States from Germany only in the late 1800s. Karl had served in the Army, so he was a little older when he started having children and, between his age and upbringing, was very "old school" about his expectations for his son.

Tommy crept up quietly to the door and inserted his key. It wouldn't turn. He tried again, but it wouldn't budge. Although Mr. Richter had never done it before, Tommy figured he had bolted the door from the inside to lock Tommy out as a punishment for being late.

Still not wanting to wake his father and endure his wrath, Tommy crept around to all of the first-floor windows, testing each one to see if one was unlocked and whether or not he could slide one up and get inside the house without having to use the door. No luck.

It was January, so Tommy could see his breath as he stood outside the house, wondering what he should do next. It had snowed earlier that week, so he could see his footprints shining in the moonlight, showing where he had just walked the entire perimeter of the house, trying to find a way to get in.

The basement windows were tiny little holes just meant for ventilation for the dryer hose, so there was no way he was going to fit through there.

Then he remembered the antenna tower. Mr. Richter was a CB radio enthusiast and had installed an antenna for both television and CB radio signal purposes, and Tommy could use the antenna tower to climb to the second floor to try to get in a window there. The only problem was that the tower was right outside of his dad's window. It was too risky.

Tommy decided that he'd "show his dad" by just sleeping on the back porch overnight. Karl Richter drove a minivan and had removed the extra bench seat and stored it on the back screened porch, so Tommy flopped onto the minivan bench as his bed for the night.

The problem was it was an unusually cold winter that January and Tommy had nothing but his coat, so about thirty minutes later, he reconsidered and decided to ring the doorbell and see what kind of trouble he was in with his dad.

He rang the doorbell and waited and gave his dad time to get down the steps and to the back door, but nothing happened. He rang again, but there was still no response. Tommy knocked then pounded on the back door, but Karl Richter never came to let his son in.

Furious that his dad would be that stubborn, Tommy went back outside, determined to force his dad to face him. It was no wonder that their last name Richter, in German, meant "judge" as Tommy felt his dad was constantly judging him. The temperature had continued to drop, so as he exited the back porch, he slid on a patch of ice that had formed on top of the snow. His feet fell out from under him, and he landed on his back. Looking up at the night sky, he saw the stars, not only the ones in the sky but also the ones from where he hit his head as a result of the fall.

After scrambling up to his feet, Tommy made his way around to the left of the house and started to climb the antenna tower. Because he had just pushed himself up from out of the snow and he wasn't wearing any gloves, his hands were cold and moist, so as he touched the metal tower, his palms instantly stuck, like a young kid sticking his tongue to a flagpole, and he winced with pain when he pulled his hand away, leaving some of the skin on the tower when he reached up for the next rung.

Finally making it up to the ledge of the second floor, still hanging onto the antenna tower, Tommy pounded on his dad's bedroom window that was just within his reach. There was no response. The curtains and shade were closed, so Tommy couldn't see inside, but he knew that Mr. Richter was in there, awake, laughing, and enjoying every minute of this "lesson" he was teaching his son about getting home late.

Sure that his dad could hear him but was ignoring him and determined to make his own point and "win" this game, Tommy decided once again that he was going to stick it out and sleep on the back porch overnight and show his dad how tough he was and that he could make it on his own.

Making his way back down the antenna tower, Tommy went back into the covered back porch. This time, he found some sheets of plastic window coverings in the corner of the porch and had an idea. He took off his winter coat, wrapped himself in the plastic window coverings, lay down on the minivan bench, and then used his winter coat as a blanket. Tired and wet from his fall in the snow, Tommy fell asleep quickly.

When the coroner arrived at the house three days later, the police officers told him that the high school had become concerned when Tommy hadn't been to school and they hadn't been able to reach his father about his absence. When the school tried calling Mr. Richter's employer, the employer had also been concerned about why Karl Richter had been a no-call, no-show for three days and had contacted the police.

The official ruling was that Tommy Richter had died at approximately 3:30 a.m. on January 27, 1978, as a result of hypothermia and was found dead on the minivan bench on the porch of the house. Karl Richter had died at approximately 10:00 p.m. on January 26, 1978, as a result of a heart condition and was found dead in his sleep on his room in the house.

The back door to the house was not bolted, but due to the extreme cold temperatures, the lock had frozen.

The house had claimed two more victims.

5

. . . .

2013

THE LAST THING Heather wanted to do was go to the house. Her mom hadn't even spoken to her in two years or let her inside of the house in ten years. But now that her mom had died, it was her responsibility to wrap things up, including the house.

Moving to Billings, Montana, had been one of the best things Heather could have done. It put distance between her and her mom. There was already emotional distance, but this put physical distance between them and provided an excuse for Heather to not have to go see her mother.

After her dad had divorced her mom when Heather was only eight, her mom became a different person. Because her mom had no friends or other social outlet and Heather was the only child, she became the target of her mom's frustration.

According to her, everything was Heather's fault. If Heather dared to say no to her mom about anything, her mom would throw a temper tantrum better than any three-year-old in the candy aisle at the grocery store. Criticism and guilt trips were like daily doses of medicine handed out over the last thirty years, which Heather's mom tried to convince her were "for her own good."

On the flight into Louisville, Heather thought about all of the secretive behavior her mother had engaged in. Throughout her whole life, her mother had constantly been telling her, "Now don't tell anybody about (fill in the blank)" as if the fact that they bought clothing at a thrift store or had a dog was a top-level high-clearance CIA security issue. She wondered what "secrets" she was going to discover when she got to the house.

Heather had gone to therapy for many years to try to make sense of her relationship with her mother. Her counselor explained that what Heather's mother was engaging in was emotional abuse. He explained that parents who physically abused children left broken bones and bruises that eventually healed, but parents who abused their children emotionally were masters of manipulation, intimidation, and guilt that left no visible marks but emotional damage that had more impact and was longer lasting.

As Heather came to learn, her mom was practically a textbook emotional abuser, applying blame for all the problems in their relationship on Heather, never resolving any of their conflicts, always trying to control the relationship, degrading her and then claiming she was "just kidding" and that Heather was "too sensitive"—the whole nine yards.

Heather's heart felt heavy as she drove the rental car toward Jeffersontown. It was just like it used to feel before her mother stopped talking to her, when she felt worn down both mentally and physically just thinking about having to deal with anything related to her mom.

As she pulled up the driveway, she saw contents of the house spewing out onto the patio and even further onto the lawn, clear evidence that a hoarder lived here. The old white frame house was now covered in white vinyl siding that was significantly worse for wear with green mold covering much of the sides. Weeds now crowded what were once beautiful flowerbeds, signs that her mom had clearly neglected the landscaping for a very long time. Nothing had changed since last time she had seen the house.

Knowing that the house was going to have to be razed, Heather's husband had told her not to worry about calling a locksmith when she got there to gain access to the house. Her mom had never given her a spare key, so her plan was to break a window in the back door and reach in to unlock the door.

The police and paramedics had twisted the knob from the inside so that it would lock when they left two weeks earlier. The mail carrier had called police when he noticed she hadn't retrieved mail out of her mailbox in a while and after noticing a foul odor emanating from the house. The coroner estimated that Heather's mother had been dead inside the house for several weeks before they discovered her body.

Heather's primary reason for even visiting the house was to ensure that there wasn't anything inside that had been her dad's that she wanted to retrieve before having the house demolished. Plus, she had wanted to arrange the demolition by phone from her home in Montana, but local officials needed her signature and a walk-through before she could authorize the Jeffersontown Fire Department to use it as a training fire site. She felt that donating it for this purpose was the least she could do to get some positive use out of the house that had been her childhood home.

Taking a deep breath and knowing what to expect when she walked through that door, Heather prepared to enter what she often referred to as "my cold Kentucky home."

It was January, so it was cold, but it felt warmer than Montana, so Heather was wearing only a midweight hoodie while she had driven from the airport. After the paramedics had removed her mother's body, the police and city had condemned the property, so all utility services had been cut off. She stuck a flashlight in the pocket of her hoodie, just in case, although it was still early afternoon, so she shouldn't need it. It was just going to be a quick walk-through and out, fifteen minutes tops, so she left her purse on the front floorboard of the rental car and plugged her cell phone into the USB port to let it charge while she was inside the house. She locked the car, stuck the keys in the other pocket of her hoodie, and started toward the house.

Outside the back screened-in porch was where the mess began. Among the many piles of garbage sitting in the snow were seventeen open garbage bags containing beanie babies. Nobody could understand that logic other than her dead mother. As she continued inside the porch, there was barely enough space to find a narrow path to get to the back door. Heather wondered how they had gotten her mother's body out among the many boxes of clothes, piles of blankets, discarded exercise equipment, spare doors, tables, bins, and bags upon bags of who-knew-what that were sitting between the porch door and the back door. Heather thought it looked like "Mount Trashmore" and that any accidental touching of any pile of crap would cause the whole intricate network of piles to come tumbling down. Looking right, Heather was pretty sure she saw what appeared to be the remains of an opossum in the far corner of the porch.

Wishing she had thought to bring a pair of work gloves or something, Heather picked up a filthy towel that was lying on the porch and wrapped it around her right hand. The back door had six panes in it, and Heather chose the one in the lowest left-hand corner to break out. It didn't break with the first punch, but then again, Heather wasn't used to punching things, but she got it the second time around. As soon as the shatters of glass began to fall, the stench started escaping through the open window, and Heather recoiled as if the smell were a physical assault. Now Heather wished she'd brought a face mask or some VapoRub or something to protect her from the horrendous odor she was going to have to endure in the ten or fifteen minutes she expected to be in the house.

Maneuvering through the now-empty panel, Heather was able to reach the doorknob on the inside and turn the toggle in order to unlock the door. As she pushed the back door open for the first time, she had to shove her entire body weight against it to get it to open against whatever pile of crap was stacked up behind it. Taking her first step in, Heather gagged and threw up in her mouth a little at the noxious mix of odors coming from inside the house. It was a mixture of mildew, decay, feces, and death. Flies swarmed past her head through the open door as if grateful for the chance to escape.

Ignoring the entryway for the moment, which offered access to the bathroom on the right and the basement to the left, Heather stared ahead to the kitchen. Straight ahead was what used to be a white stove, now dirty and rusted in spots. Piled high on top of the stove were pill bottles, cast-iron skillets, empty butter dishes, Krispy Kreme donut boxes, stacks of mail, and discarded jewelry. To the left of the stove was a microwave cart, which was inaccessible due to piles of boxes and junk in front of it, and lying on top of the microwave were stacks of mail, dishes, clothes, telephone books, and a radio. To the right of the stove was an old cabinet where they used to store canned goods when Heather was a child. Formerly white, it was now covered in food stains, and lying on top of the cabinet was a broken coffeepot, another radio, and a pile of three or four inches of papers. Sadly, that was the cleanest and neatest part of kitchen.

It looked as though Heather's mom had given up on using garbage cans and had been throwing her trash on the floor for quite some time. Ice cream containers, cereal boxes, canned food, and fast-food bags littered the kitchen floor.

The countertops were piled at least nine inches high with every kind of thing imaginable in another version of the back porch's "Mount Trashmore." Empty cookie tins, discarded takeout containers, giveaway bank calendars, empty soda cans, egg cartons, hair brushes, another radio, and portable phones were among the hundreds of items piled up on both sides of the sink. In the sink were a stack of dirty dishes and a handful of potato peels. Looking up, the curtains above the sink, though white, appeared black, as they were covered with gnats that flittered from the sink to the curtains and now appeared to be interested in Heather's eyes. She swatted at them and moved on to the dining room.

The dining room was less of a health hazard, but still a mess. Four to five inches of thick greasy dust covered everything in the room. Various items were strewn across the floor. The dining room table and an old buffet were covered with clothing, baskets, dolls, and assorted items, and boxes and bags filled all available space in the room.

Heather moved on to the parlor. She wasn't prepared for what she saw. She knew that her mother had stopped sleeping in the upstairs bedroom, but she wasn't expecting to see the dramatic horrific set of circumstances in which her mother had been sleeping.

A small bed had been set up in the corner of the parlor. There were no sheets on the bed, and the mattresses were well-worn and covered in stains, both urine as well as human sweat. The floors had been stripped bare to the subflooring plywood and were covered in filth, food, trash, and stains. She must have had a cat at some point because there was a litter box nearby overflowing with cat poop and several plastic grocery-store bags full of cat poop sitting next to the litter box, just three feet from the bed. Heather wondered if she was going to find a dead cat.

Near the bed was a portable potty filled with human waste, and Heather once again gagged and threw up in her mouth for a minute.

Just like the other rooms, this room was filled with piles of items: a guitar, an old suitcase, bags, clothes, shoes, old 78-rpm records, dusty and torn yard-sale books, lamps, Christmas decorations, and more.

Shaking her head, Heather looked toward the staircase. It was totally blocked at the bottom with old rolled-up rugs, a fan, an old oxygen tank, picture frames, and wrapping paper. Knowing she needed to check upstairs to see if any of her father's belongings were there, Heather pushed aside the rugs, causing a huge wave of dust to fly up in the air and three mice to run out from underneath the pile and across the floor. Choking down dust, Heather wished she'd brought her bottle of water inside with her, but she just coughed and started her way up the stairs.

Looking into the upstairs bedrooms was like looking into a completely different house. Behind those closed doors were clean and simple bedrooms with the same furniture that Heather had remembered from her childhood. She sat on the bed in the room that had been her father's and remembered how the room used to smell like Old Spice aftershave after he'd leave for work. Her dad was the best and had died much too young, and she missed him. Looking through the closet and the dresser drawers in that room, Heather found nothing of her father's and moved on to the next room.

The bedroom closest to the upstairs bathroom was a guest bedroom and was completely empty except for the furniture. She closed that door and went to the final bedroom.

The small bedroom closest to the stairs had been Heather's bedroom as a child. It was very different because instead of the usual cornered ceiling, it had a rounded ceiling. It was the only bedroom in the front of the house, and she had always liked looking out at the magnificent magnolia trees. It was also the bedroom the farthest away from the railroad track, so it was the quietest. The closet in that bedroom was also unique because it had a second area of storage adjacent to it, sort of like a little cave, and Heather had used her imagination as a child and played in that closet many times to hide from her mother when she was young. Finding nothing there but memories, Heather closed that door and made her way back downstairs.

The only thing left to check was the basement. Her family had always called it a basement, but it wasn't really what most people would call a basement. To get to it, there was a door in the floor of the entryway inside the back door that you had to lift a door with a pulley-and-lever system. It was a heavy door, and once lifted, you walked down a dozen or so concrete steps. Half of the area downstairs was concrete, onto which the washer, dryer, furnace, and water heater had been installed, and the other half was earth floor with stone and earth walls, more like a cellar. There were also earth crawlspaces where the ductwork and electrical work had been installed. When there was electricity, there were two single light bulbs to illuminate the basement. There were two small windows for ventilation. As a child, whenever there had been tornadoes or severe storms, Heather had been made to go down to the basement to ride out the storm. She hated the basement. She had always dreaded going down there to do the laundry. It was a scary place, cold and musty, and she would always run back upstairs as quickly as possible after shoving the clothes in the washer or dryer. She always thought something was going to come out at her from the crawlspaces or the small earthen room in the front where her mother had stored food she had canned fresh from the garden.

Heather walked to the entryway and stared at the basement door. Above where the door would swing back to the left and rest when opened were two bracket shelves. Those shelves were full of paint cans, artificial flowers, vases, an old wall mirror, curtain rods, and an amalgam of objects both useless and outdated. She had to move a hamper and two buckets of junk off the cellar door in order to reach the piece of metal that latched the door in place. Then she reached up to grab the old rope pulley system to raise the heavy door. The door creaked and moaned as its weight was lifted, and Heather propped the door up against the wall beneath the shelves, grabbed the flashlight out of her hoodie pocket, and headed down the concrete stairs.

There were boxes stored down here as well. She decided to start in the back and work her way out of the basement quickly. In the first set of boxes she found four Crock-Pots, all broken. Glancing through the next couple of boxes, she saw that they too contained broken small appliances and kitchenware.

Looking up on the concrete wall in the back of the basement, Heather saw some old license plates that her dad had saved. She smiled, but those weren't worth keeping. Shoved back in the crawlspace were some old fishing poles, some older model rods and reels, and one cane pole. She remembered that her dad and uncles used to fish together once a year up in Northeastern Kentucky on the Licking River. Seeing those fishing poles evoked memories of those childhood trips and fun times with family. They wouldn't be worth keeping, but she was glad to have seen them again.

At that moment, a train passed by the house. Even though Heather hadn't lived there in years, she could remember all the years of living next to a railroad track. People used to ask her how she could stand all the constant noise, but she'd explain that you just get used to it and tune it out. This train sounded like a long one as it had more than one engine, so she continued about her work of looking through the boxes and ignored the loud noise of the train passing by.

It was unfortunate for Heather that she was able to tune out the noise.

Vibrations from the trains over the many years combined with the deteriorated state of the house proved to be a bad combination during the time that the train passed by the house. The only remaining screw that was holding the mounting hardware for the pulley system of the basement door was vibrated out of the rotting ceiling by the heavy motors of the passing train, causing the tension to release and the heavy door to drop and slam slut. The tremendous force of the slamming door resulted in a chain reaction in the bracket shelves above the door, and all of the contents started cascading off the shelf like a junkyard waterfall. Heavy cans of unopened paint plopped on top of the cellar door, vases tumbled and shattered, and the wall mirror fell off the top shelf, spewing glass everywhere. An ironing board that had been propped up in the corner fell, wedging itself between the door and the wooden banister above. Heather didn't know it yet, but she was trapped in the basement.

At the end of the concrete wall to the left of the clothes dryer, Heather finally hit a jackpot. The box contained mementos of her childhood. Pointing her flashlight down inside the aging cardboard container, Heather saw things she remembered making in kindergarten and elementary school. She sat down on the cold concrete and started to pull items out of the box one at a time. First was the plaster of paris handprint she had made in kindergarten and scribbled her name underneath. Next was the oddly shaped blue clay pottery piece that was supposed to have been an ashtray that she had made in first grade. She pulled out the disintegrating brightly colored maraca that she had made in third grade out of a broken light bulb wrapped in papier mâché and then painted. A sentimental warm feeling filled Heather's heart that she hadn't felt in many years. She decided just to take the whole box with her and sort through it more in the hotel room and got up to carry it over to the bottom of the basement stairs so that it would be ready to carry up when she left.

When she got to the bottom of the stairs, she realized the cellar door had shut. Assuming the propped-up door had just lost its grip and fallen down and that she hadn't heard it during the train's passing, Heather calmly walked up the stairs to push the basement door back up. It didn't budge. She pushed harder, but there was still no movement on the part of the cellar door. What the hell?

With both hands palms up over her head against the cellar door, she pushed with all her strength to no avail. Deciding she needed more force, she bent over to the left and ran up at the door with her right shoulder. The door budged, barely an eighth of an inch, but it budged, and she could then hear the glass and debris shaking when the door came back down and the weight of things rolling around on the door when it shut. It was then that she realized what must have happened to cause the cellar door to close, and it was also about that time that her shoulder started scream-ing out in pain at her.

Grabbing her shoulder with her left hand and walking back down the stairs, Heather doubled over in pain from where she had so stupidly thought she was somebody who could ram her body into doors and bust through them. Rubbing her shoulder, she thought, *That's gonna leave a bruise.*

She reached into the pocket of her hoodie to grab her cell phone to call for help, but it wasn't there. She searched her jean pockets, and it wasn't there either. Then she remembered that she'd put it on the charger in the rental car. *Damn it!*

Normally an analytical person who would think through all her options, Heather was claustrophobic, so she was already starting to get the anxiety associated with the fear of having no escape.

Realizing how much crap had fallen on top of the cellar door and her slim chances of being able to lift it, Heather had to look at other options. There were two small win-dows in the basement. She walked over to the one behind the washing machine. It was up about five feet above the floor and was a crank-out window. As she tried cranking the window open, the rusted crank broke away from the window assembly. Frustrated, Heather went back to the rear of the basement where she had seen the fishing poles and took one of them to smash out the glass in the small one-foot-by-three-foot window.

Realizing that there was no way she was going to fit through the window, Heather started yelling out the opening for help, though the chances of anyone hearing her cries were slim to none on this dead-end street with the nearest neighbor more than a mile away. Recognizing that her yells were futile, Heather pondered on what her other options might be.

She wondered whether or not she could get the basement door to budge up enough again to possibly wedge in one of the fishing poles and use it like a lever to force it open. Going back up the stairs with the fiberglass fishing rod, Heather tried once again to push up on the heavy wooden cellar door with no success.

There had to be something down in the basement that she could use to force that door open, so she started on a search of the areas she hadn't yet explored. With the broken window now letting in the cold air, Heather hugged herself and rubbed her arms to warm up a little and then set about to find something to work her way out of the basement.

There was nothing really in the open area by the washing machine except for the open window, the furnace, and the hot water heater. The only place left to look was the small earthen room by the stairs. Heather hated that room more than any other part of the basement. It had coarse rock and earth walls that scratched you when you accidentally rubbed against them and a dirt floor. It smelled musty in there, and there were crawlspaces that she didn't know where they led. There were random items like vintage bottles lying on top of the rock walls in the small earthen room. It was very dark in that windowless room, and even with her flashlight, Heather couldn't make out what larger items were taking up space in there. She honed the light onto the shelves, hoping she'd find a tool of some sort, and something flashed silver. It was an old rasp. The tip was missing, but it had a long steel bar going into a wooden handle. She didn't plan to rasp the cellar door, but if she could wedge the end of the steel bar into the door's opening, perhaps she could use it to lift the door. It was worth a try.

Taking a deep breath, Heather inserted the end of the rasp into the opening between the door and the concrete wall at the opening of the cellar and pried hard on its wooden handle. Moaning and creaking, the door moved just enough so that Heather could see that the ironing board had wedged itself between the cellar door and the banister, preventing the door from being opened any further. She could also see the broken ceramics and items that had fallen from the shelves above the basement door and splashes of primer indicating that the buckets of paint had fallen as well. Then the wooden handle of the rasp snapped away from the steel bar, sending Heather reeling backward down the concrete steps.

Unsure of how long she had blacked out, Heather awoke to pure darkness. Panicking, she reached for her flashlight but it wasn't in the pocket of her hoodie. Where had it gone? She reached around the concrete floor where she was lying at the bottom of the concrete stairs. It wasn't there. Her left hand ran across something sticky and viscous, and she pulled it back in disgust. She sat up, disoriented. Why was everything so dark? She was seeing stars, both literally and figuratively. Head throbbing, Heather realized she was looking out the open window of the basement and seeing stars overhead. It was nighttime! Head throbbing, Heather realized she was seeing stars also because her head was injured. Reaching up to touch where the pain was, Heather once again felt something sticky and viscous. It was blood—her blood. The blood was coming from her head. She must have hit her head on the concrete stairs when the rasp broke, sending her reeling backward down them.

Blinking her eyes to make the stars disappear, Heather heard a sound to her right. It sounded like it was coming from behind the washing machine. With no flashlight and only a small amount of moonlight coming through the window opening to provide any illumination to the dreary basement, Heather stood up and walked over to find out what was causing the noise.

When she moved, though, whatever it was moved too, running past her, skimming her leg as it passed. Shivers went down Heather's spine. What fresh hell was this? Then she realized that a wild animal must have come through the broken window from the cold into the only-slightly-warmer basement while she was knocked out cold.

Heather stood there shaking her head. She remembered what her husband had often told her: "No good deed goes unpunished." She could have just stayed in Montana and let her mother's house fall down on its own. After all, what had her mother ever done for her? Nothing she'd ever done for her mother had ever been good enough and certainly, in her mother's eyes, she'd never been good enough. Everything she'd ever tried to do to help her mom had ended up being a pain in the rear and causing her more trouble somehow in the end. It looked as though even in death her mother was still going to cause her more trouble than it was worth to try to dispose of this house.

Now here she was trapped in the basement of this house from hell, head bleeding, body freezing, thirsty, with some animal lurking nearby, and no idea of how she was going to escape from this predicament. Heather's heart was still pounding, and she groaned as she took a deep breath. Her torso fell forward as she momentarily lost her balance.

Think, Heather, think. Should I throw items out the window and somebody will notice? Yeah, right, like somebody's gonna notice a bunch of a junk in a junk-filled yard at an empty house on a dead-end street. Next idea?

Walking back toward the stairs with the intention of sitting down, Heather stepped on something that rolled underneath her foot. It was her flashlight! She reached down and picked it up and tried the button. It still worked! That inspired Heather with a new idea for her rescue. She made her way over to the open window, shivering as she stood against the blowing wind, and starting shining her flashlight outside in the vain hope that someone would pass by and see its signal.

Really, Heather? And just who is going to be walking down the railroad tracks to see the weak little light from this flashlight? Hold on, what if I wait until the next train passes and try to signal the engineer? Yes, that's what I'll do.

Heather retreated from the window to wait for the next train to pass to try to her flashlight idea. In the meantime she thought she might try looking through some more boxes to see if she could find anything useful that could help her out of this mess.

She took her flashlight and went back to the rear of the basement where she had started to see if she had overlooked anything in her initial review of the boxes. She scanned again and saw the same discarded appliances and junk. Looking up again at the license plates her dad had saved, she glanced at some other items sitting on a shelf nearby that she hadn't noticed before. Sitting on the shelf was an old lighter of her father's. It was a collector's item World War II era Zippo lighter, the kind that was made out of black crackle finished steel because metal was in short supply during the war. It had the US Air Force insignia on it. Her dad was proud of that lighter because he too had served in the Air Force. Heather used to enjoy the pungent smell of the lighter fluid when her dad would smoke the occasional King Edward cigar when she was little.

Picking up the Zippo, several ideas passed through Heather's mind. *I could set the wooden door on fire, and it'll burn through, and I can get up the basement stairs. Really, genius? And that won't set the whole house on fire or the debris won't fall in on you and block your egress from the house? Okay, then how about I set something on fire in the basement and let the smoke billow out the window and then someone will see the smoke and come and rescue me? Better, but how will you control the fire, and won't the smoke overcome you in this small contained space? Come on, Heather, think! I've got it! I'll set something on fire and throw it out the window, and the smoke will be outside, and it will draw someone's attention, and they will come to check it out. It's January, genius. Won't they just think it's a fireplace smoking somewhere and ignore it? Damn it!*

As she pondered her dilemma, Heather heard a weird hissing noise up and to her left and then another noise, almost like sneezing, down and to her left. She swung around and aimed her flashlight to see one young opossum hanging by its tail from a rafter hissing at her and another young opossum beneath it making the strange sneezing noise. Their eyes shone back at her like a deer caught in the headlights. It must have been because she was staring at them too that Heather didn't see the mama opossum coming at her from the right until it clamped down firmly on her leg with its razor-sharp claws. As she screamed and kicked her leg to try to shake it loose, the mama opossum only tightened her grip further and starting shimmying up Heather's body like it was climbing up a tree. The young opossums hissed as if applauding their mother's heroic actions to protect them. The mama opossum started hissing as if talking trash to Heather like she's getting ready to open a can of whoop ass on her. It was a fifteen-pound opossum with a hundred pounds of attitude.

Heather reached down with both hands, trying to grab the maniacal marsupial, but it ripped at her hands with its incisors, shredding the skin nearly to the bone before it unclenched its jaw and started once again racing up her torso.

Throwing her hands up to cover her face and turning her head, Heather was unable to protect the vein in her body most vulnerable to attack, and the mama opossum ripped her canines into her jugular. Blood spurted out in a wide radius while Heather fell to the ground.

Thankfully, Heather was once again rendered unconscious when hitting the concrete floor as the opossum family began its all-you-can-eat buffet.

The house had claimed two more victims.

6

BACK AT THE LIAR'S BENCH

OVER THE ONE hundred plus years that the house had existed, there had been twelve owners. All the previous owners of the home as well as all their children were deceased.

"Every single person who has ever lived in that house has died in that house," Haskell explained to his buddies. "And I know why."

The first settlers in Kentucky in the 1750s and 1760s had brought their slaves with them. The early settlement stations that were developed relied on slave labor as they expanded. When the slaves would die, rather than be buried with the settlers, they were taken to separate areas to be buried in unmarked mass graves. In this area, the designated area for the slaves to be buried was in a plot of land later to be known as Hubertson on Edington Lane in Jeffersontown, Kentucky.

The Commonwealth of Kentucky had chartered the Louisville and Nashville Railroad in 1850. It was well-known that railroads being built before the Civil War that were east of the Mississippi and south of the Mason-Dixon line used slave labor to construct the tracks that would be used to expand the rail lines. In those days, slaves were considered the cheapest and most reliable labor. They formed the majority of the South's railway labor force.

Up and down the South, African Americans would lift a lining bar and force it into a ballast. Because of the force needed to throw the lining bar, the workers would make a "huh" sound when releasing the weight of the bar. It was common for the crews to sing work songs to keep in rhythm with specific tasks. The crew leader would start the chant with specific directions for his crew to perform a task such as realigning a rail to a specific position, and the crew would chant back a response. The songs were both utilitarian as well as helpful in keeping up the mood of the workers. These mournful, melodic songs could be heard up and down the tracks all day long.

Railroad construction crews were not only subjected to extreme weather conditions but they also had to lay tracks across and through many difficult natural geographical features such as rock, rivers, and creeks. Other dangers of railroad life included wildlife attacks, rockslides, malnutrition, and disease. Roughly one out of every three hundred slave railroad workers died laying tracks in the South.

Whenever workers died, the foremen would have their bodies hauled onto railcars to be taken to one central spot to be buried in a mass grave. Rather than have bodies strewn all up and down the line, the railway had one place to throw the bodies. Knowing that a slave mass burial site already existed in this portion of the county from a century earlier, the railroad carried the bodies of the hundreds of workers who died to a plot of land later to be known as Hubertson on Edington Lane in Jeffersontown, Kentucky. No families were notified, no gravestones were erected, no prayers were said, and no grief was had.

Haskell had heard tales that sometimes people could hear the souls of the dead slaves singing from their graves beneath the land. He had also heard of problems on plots of land in other parts of the state where slaves had been buried in mass graves. They had determined in Logan County, Kentucky, that beneath a home where an inordinate number of deaths had occurred was a slave burial ground. The scary part was that the number of deaths that had occurred in the house was the exact number of bodies buried beneath the land.

The problem was that the house on Edington Avenue had been demolished several years ago, and the lot had just recently been sold. A developer was seeking to build a hundred-unit apartment building on that site.

Haskell felt it was important to tell someone now about the history of the property because he was sure that it wasn't the house itself but anything that would ever be built on that land would be impacted. He shuddered in horror at the thought of how many bodies might be buried at Hubertson and how many deaths could happen inside the walls of those hundred-apartment units. That property would be a death sentence for anyone who lived there.

This was worse than anything Haskell had ever experienced in his twenty-five years as a railroad detective.

Epilogue

· · · · · · · · · · · · · · · · · · · ·

THE MAYOR DUTIFULLY smiled for the camera as he used the comically large scissors to cut the ceremonial ribbon marking the opening of the Edington Estates. Several members of the Jeffersontown City Council had put in an appearance as well as they were always so good about supporting local businesses.

These luxury apartments were two- and three-bedroom units built on the end of Edington Avenue next to the railroad track. The developer was thrilled that 80 percent of them were preleased, and renters would start moving in within the next week. He expected the apartments to be 100 percent occupied within three months of opening, a record-breaker for any development he had ever done.

Haskell had passed away in his sleep six months earlier, and his buddies had written off his tale about the slave burial ground on Edington Avenue as just another one of his famous embellishments. Sure, there had been a few unfortunate deaths that they could remember in that house, but surely it was just coincidence.

As the reporters and crowd walked away from the ribbon-cutting ceremony, some could swear that they heard singing.